CHAPTER 1
Magic at the Farmers' Market

"You're it!" Hailey called triumphantly, finally having caught up with her friend Camie as she climbed the ladder up to the playground slide.

Today was the opening day for the Carnation Farmers' Market. Hailey and her brother Rowan were playing tag with their friends at the playground right by the market booths. Hailey and Camie had just finished dancing the maypole with the other children. The kids' maypole had become an opening day tradition at the market over the past few years, and they always looked forward to weaving their flower crowns and twirling the colorful silky ribbons around the pole on the lawn. They loved the live music that accompanied their dancing.

Farmers' market days were always the best days at the Carnation playground too, because all the kids played there. Today, Rowan, Sarah, Hailey, and Camie had found their friends Juniper, Dain, Skyla, and Katie, and they were having a great game of playground tag. Camie's little sister Lizzy was there too. Now Camie was it, and she was pulling her way up the slide after Juniper. When Juniper put her hand on the bar  at the top of the slide to pull herself up, she screamed and started to cry. In her hurry to get away from Camie she hadn't noticed the bumblebee on the bar.

The game of tag came to a quick end as the friends gathered around Juniper. "I'll get some plantain," said Rowan. "That will take the sting out of it." He began to search around the playground. Hailey, Sarah, and Camie joined in the search, but there seemed to be no plantain around that was clean enough to chew up to make a poultice.

Then the children heard a little voice calling out, "Over here!" It sounded so tiny they were surprised they could even

Herb Fairies

A Magical Tale of Plants & Their Remedies

When four young friends discover an herb fairy at the park, they are drawn into an adventure beyond their wildest dreams. The Old Man of the Forest has cast a terrible spell, locking up much of the plant magic in the world. The Herb Fairies turn to the children for help, and everyone discovers that the only way to restore the magic is by working together. By the end of this thirteen book series, readers become keepers of plant medicine magic.

Join the Herb Fairies Book Club!

Herb Fairies is a complete herbal learning system for kids.
For each of the thirteen books in the Herb Fairies series...

Draw and write about what you learned in your very own Magic Keeper's Journal.

Make the herbal remedies and recipes the kids make in the books with Recipe Cards!

Learn with puzzles, stories, songs, recipes, poems and games in Herbal Roots zine.

Color your favorite fairies or print out posters to hang on your bedroom wall.

Book club membership gives you access to the complete learning system on our mobile optimized site. Also includes audio books read by Kimberly, printable books and eBook versions for Kindle, iPad and other devices.

Visit HerbFairies.com

LearningHerbs

Herb Fairies
Book Three: A Fairy Festival Surprise

Written by Kimberly Gallagher
Illustrated by Swapan Debnath
Produced by John M. Gallagher

If you are not sure what a word means or how it is pronounced, check the glossary in the back of the book.

Special Thanks to my mom, Cheryl Delmonte, a fellow writer, who has always encouraged my love for the craft of weaving stories for others to enjoy.

Special Thanks to Maryann Gallagher Agostin, Hailey Gallagher, Rowan Gallagher, Rosalee de la Forêt, and the LearningHerbs community.

The herbal and plant information in Herb Fairies is for educational purposes only. The information within the Herb Fairies books and activities are not intended as a substitute for the advice provided by your physician or other medical professional. Always consult with a health care practitioner before using any herbal remedy or food, especially if pregnant, nursing, or have a medical condition.

ISBN: 978-1-938419-29-4

Published by LearningHerbs.com, LLC, Shelton, WA.
LearningHerbs and Herb Fairies logos are registered trademarks of LearningHerbs.com, LLC.
Herb Fairies is a registered trademark of LearningHerbs.com, LLC.
First print edition, January 2017. Published and printed in the U.S.A. on FSC® certified paper.

The Herb Fairies series is dedicated to the memory of
James Joseph Gallagher, Sr.

For Rowan and Hailey...

hear it over all the playground noise. It was coming from the back corner near the fence. There was a little overgrown area back there with a rosebush protecting it.

Sure enough, when they looked down by the bush's roots there was a nice healthy plantain plant, and standing beside it was a tiny fairy no taller than Camie's six-year-old hand. The fairy was smiling at them and holding up a beautiful leaf of plantain. Sarah reached out for it, her eyes shining. All the children were excited to have found another herb fairy. Sarah and Rowan rushed over to Juniper to help her with her bee sting.

"Thank you for helping us find the plantain," said Camie to the little fairy.

"Are you the plantain fairy?" asked Hailey.

"Yes, I am," said the fairy. "I am Tago."

About this time, Rowan and Sarah returned from helping Juniper. "Thanks for helping us find that plantain," said Rowan. "Our friend Juniper is feeling much better now."

Tago did indeed look like a plantain fairy. He was stocky and muscular with a prominent nose and angular chin. His brown hair was tousled under his cap, and his green eyes sparkled with merriment and a little bit of mischief. He had on a ragged green suit with fine white stripes, and worn boots with one sole hanging loose. In his ample, healing hands he carried a plantain seed stalk with a little pouch hanging off of it over his shoulder. His golden wings were oval shaped, just like the leaves of a plantain plant. He looked like a friendly hobo, ready to hitch a ride on the next train through town.

"I'm glad you kids knew to look for plantain to help Juniper with her bee sting," said Tago.

"It works so well," said Rowan. "Juniper stopped crying immediately, and I knew it had taken the sting away just like it always does for me."

"Do you need our help in the Fairy Herb Garden again?" asked Sarah hopefully. All the children loved their fairy adventures and they were eager to help out again if they could.

"Well, not exactly," said Tago. At the children's disappointed looks, Tago hurried on, "You see, today is the beginning of our spring festival, and we wanted to bring you children to the garden so you could be part of the party. We thought it would be a good way to thank you for all of your help."

"Really?" squealed Hailey with delight. She loved the idea of joining in a fairy festival.

"Spring is our favorite season in the Fairy Herb Garden," said Tago. "All the plants are green and growing again and so many flowers are blooming. All the fairies cook up their favorite foods and we play music and dance and sing."

"It sounds beautiful!" sighed Sarah.

"I can't wait to get there," said Camie. "Do you have the fairy dust to take us with you?"

"Indeed I do," said Tago, "but we'd best find a more private place for sprinkling it. All these people will be pretty surprised if you all just disappear."

"Oh, right," said Rowan. He led everyone over to the tunnel slide. All four children scrambled inside and out of sight. Tago flew over the top of them and sprinkled the fairy dust. They began to tingle and shrink and the gentle wind swirled around them, taking them to the Fairy Herb Garden once more.

CHAPTER 2
Spring Festival

"Wow! Oh my gosh. It's so beautiful!" all the children exclaimed at once. They spun around, taking in the amazing beauty of the Fairy Herb Garden all decorated for the fairies' spring festival. The spiders had spun webs which were then decorated with flowers to make beautiful garlands all around the festival area. There was a table loaded with delicious-looking food that smelled absolutely amazing. Some of the fairies had set up little booths where they were trading their goodies. Stellaria was there with some delicious-looking chickweed bread, and the children recognized Viola, who had made her special candied violet flowers.

In the center of the area was the fairy maypole. It was a strong twig of cedar, nearly twelve inches tall, and instead of ribbon, the fairies had hung vining plants from its top. They were dangling loose, ready to be woven in the maypole dance. There was a flowing fountain at one edge of the festivities, and in front of the fountain was a large, ornate silver platter heaped with goodies and flowers.

Fairies were everywhere. Some were playing games like berry toss and fairy tag. Others were twirling and flipping in the air above the children's heads, or sampling some of the goodies from the tables and fairy booths. The children saw that Trust and Awareness, the two trolls that they'd helped to heal, were there among the fairies. It looked like Trust was leading some games involving blindfolds and Awareness had the fairies trying to sneak up on each other and grab a flower petal without being noticed.

There was a great deal of laughter and talk, but still the children could hear the sweet sound of fairy music drifting on the air. The gentle, vibrant sounds of the stringed instruments and fairy flutes mingled with the delicious smells of the food and flowers and washed over the children in a wave of nourishing beauty.

Hailey found herself smiling broadly, and even laughing with joy.

Tago saw the children's obvious delight and was excited that he had managed to find them and bring them to the festival. "Come this way," Tago urged. "I think Dandy is about to announce the beginning of the aerial acrobatics show."

Sure enough, as they followed Tago they caught a glimpse of Dandy standing high on a flat-topped rock calling the fairies together to watch the upcoming performance. The children watched in amazement as a group of fairies, all dressed in tight-fitting, colorful suits, performed aerial flips and dives and twirls and twists in a complicated, choreographed pattern.

The result was like living fireworks, shooting up and exploding with awe-inspiring beauty. The performance mesmerized everyone watching, the fairy music and aerial acrobatics carrying them into a dream of color and sweet sensation.

None of the children knew how long they watched, but as the show wound down and Tago and Viola approached them with a tray full of delicious fairy snacks, they realized that they had grown hungry. Another fairy had come along with Viola. She was dressed equally beautifully in a petal skirt of purple, blue, and white, and none of the children were surprised when Viola introduced her as her sister, Pansy.

"I'm glad I get to meet you this time," Pansy said. "I hope you'll be able to stay to watch the dancing later. Viola and I have been practicing for months. We're really excited about our dance this year."

Camie and Hailey's eyes lit up at the prospect of seeing the fairy dance. Their own ballet recital was coming up soon, and they knew how exciting it was to prepare and to perform.

"Oh, I hope so too!" exclaimed Camie. "This is such a magical day. Your spring festival is so exciting."

"We're glad you're enjoying it," laughed Viola.

While the children ate, Tago and Viola explained how the spring festival was a time for the fairies to celebrate the return of life and beauty to the Fairy Herb Garden. They all prepared their favorite fairy treats and entertained each other with performances. Sometimes fairies would bring exciting news about something that they were working on in the year to come—a new recipe, a new idea for a game or dance, that kind of thing. And always, they prepared the silver platter with their very favorite things as a gift to the May Queen.

"The tree fairies say they can remember when the queen would come to the fairy festival," said Viola. "At sunset, when the maypole dance would begin, she would step out of the forest, crowned in flowers and wearing her beautiful, shimmering rainbow robe. She would stay and dance and laugh and play among the fairies until late into the night."

"Our party still goes on until the middle of the night," said Tago, "but I think those fairies are just making up the story about the May Queen."

"The silver tray always disappears, though," said Pansy. "It's returned empty early the next morning."

A little boy fairy dressed in a purple and yellow suit came running up. "Hey, Viola," he said. "Want to play tag?"

Viola introduced the boy as her little brother Johnny. "His plant is the johnny-jump-up," she explained. "He certainly is a little jumper too—always running and playing."

"I'll play tag with you," Rowan offered, "but I can't fly." Rowan had noticed that the fairy tag game was played mostly in the air. "Do you think we could find some fairies that wouldn't mind a game on the ground?"

It wasn't long before the children had engaged a whole group of fairies in a game of running tag. The fairies were not used to moving on the ground, so the children did quite well even though they were in unfamiliar territory. They all ran and played and laughed together until they heard Dandy ringing a bell and calling everyone together for the great feast.

All the fairies held hands and formed a giant circle. When they'd settled into their places, an elderly grandmother fairy with twinkling eyes and wearing a beautiful hawthorn flower crown stepped forward. She gave thanks for another year of flowers and greenery returning to the garden and for all the wonderful treats they had to share with one another. She gave a special thank-you to the children who had been coming to help the fairies and trolls. The children blushed as the fairies all looked in their direction with smiles of gratitude.

Then the feast began. Everyone filled their plates from the wonderful array of food on the long table. The children had never tasted so many delicious things in one meal. There were herbed breads and butters, rose petal and chamomile honeys, berry juices, and wild salads decorated with colorful flower petals and dressed with delicious herbal dressings. There were dandelion fritters and cattail shoot quiches, buttery, sweet soups, and even fizzy hawthorn flower soda.

For dessert there were cakes decorated with edible flowers—violets, pansies, chamomile, and hawthorn. There were rhubarb pies and dandelion flower cookies. Everyone ate until they were full and then ate some more, and still there was food left on that incredible table. The snacking would continue until late into the night as the festival went on and on.

As the fairies and children began to feel they could eat no more, the sun began to set, and everyone gathered round the maypole. The music began again, and as the sun turned the sky vibrant shades of orange and pink the fairies danced the maypole, weaving under and over one another so that the vines were woven beautifully around the cedar pole. Some of those who weren't dancing gazed off into the

woods, hoping against hope that the May Queen would emerge from the forest of green.

It was quite a surprise, then, when a loud troll voice and stomping interrupted the music and laughter. "Oh! Owwwwwww, owww, owww!" The troll came blundering out of the forest and into the circle of fairies holding out his hand, which was littered with devil's club thorns.

CHAPTER 3
Plantain Healing

At first the troll was so distracted by the pain in his hand that he didn't notice he was suddenly surrounded by fairies. When he did notice, his eyes grew wide and wild with fear and his howls of pain turned to screams of panic. "Ahhhhhhhh! Fairies! Get me out of here!" He turned in circles, knocking over booths and decorations and even running into the maypole. It only came up to his knee, but he yelled in pain and grabbed his shin with his good hand and began hopping around, trying to get back to the forest.

Everyone cleared a path for him, seeing that it would be impossible to calm him down until he reached some place where he felt safer. The troll ran quickly back under the cover of the trees. Trust and Awareness were fast on his heels, and the children followed as quickly as their tiny fairy legs would take them. Tago flew along with the children. He'd seen the splinters in the troll's hand and had a hunch they would soon need some plantain healing.

Trust and Awareness caught up with this new troll quickly, since he became lost in a coughing fit and had to stop running. The troll straightened up and looked at the two who had now taken hold of his arms. His eyes grew wide with wonder and they could see that he had a flash of a memory before his eyes clouded once more with pain and panic.

"It's okay now," soothed Trust. "Catch your breath."

"Yes," said Awareness. "The children are here. They will help you."

"Children?" queried the new troll.

"That's right," answered Trust. She could see that he was remembering the words that had come to Trust when she had met the children a couple of months before: "The children must answer the riddle to guess your name." These words were somewhere in the swirl of confusion in the minds of all sick trolls.

This troll was just realizing that he really didn't remember his name when the children arrived with Tago. The plantain fairy had already managed to find a few plantain leaves and flew forward with them, eager to offer his help. When the troll saw the fairy, he began to struggle against the hands that held him in place. "No!" he shouted. "Let me go. I've got to get away from that fairy!"

"It's okay," Trust repeated. "He's come to help. Really. I know it's hard to believe, but Awareness and I have come to trust the fairies."

"Yes," said Awareness. "Please stop trying to run. It's obvious you're not in good shape. Let us help you."

The new troll began coughing again. He finally fell to the ground, cradling his sore, splintered hand.

"That's it," said Sarah, bravely stepping forward. "We really do want to help."

"Yes," said Rowan. "I bet we can get a lot of those splinters out right away with our tiny, fairy-sized hands. Will you let us try?"

Slowly, cautiously, the troll lowered his hand to the ground. The children gathered around and began carefully removing the devil's club thorns. Tago helped as well. Rowan had been right. Their fairy-sized hands acted as tweezers and they were able to remove many of the thorns.

"Oh, owwww. It still hurts," complained the troll when the children had removed as many as they could.

"Yes," said Rowan, "there are quite a few we couldn't get. They are in too deep, and it's hard to see in the moonlight."

"Oh no!" wailed the troll. "What will we do?"

"Plantain will help draw them out," Hailey said.

"Yes, indeed," agreed Tago. "The poultices will work better if they are warm, though. Can we go over to my house? It's a huge patch of plantain, and I can warm them easily there."

Reluctantly, the troll agreed to follow them to Tago's house. It helped when Tago explained that he lived on the edge of the garden, so the troll wouldn't have to go in among the other fairies.

"Plantain grows best in disturbed areas where the soil isn't very rich," Tago explained. "So my patch is on the edge of the garden, on one of the old paths that used to lead into the Enchanted Forest. Plantain is great at drawing nutrients up from deep in the soil, just like it's great at drawing splinters out from deep in the skin." Tago talked as they walked, distracting the troll from his pain and his fear of the fairies.

Luckily, the moon was nearly full that night and they could see their way on the path pretty easily. When they arrived at Tago's home, Sarah helped the troll sit down in a clear spot on the path next to the plantain patch.

The children began to gather plantain leaves for the poultices. Hailey and Rowan helped Sarah and Camie to identify the oval-shaped leaves with long parallel veins. Tago emerged from his house with a mortar and pestle. When the leaves had been mashed up, he and Hailey went inside to heat the poultices, leaving the others to keep the troll company. Soon Tago and Hailey brought out the warm poultices, and the troll reluctantly lowered his hand to the ground so the children could put them on.

"Of course," said Sarah, sighing. "More sticky, gooey green stuff."

The troll wasn't too excited about the whole idea either, but the tension in his face eased as the plantain soothed the pain of the splinters and began to pull them toward the surface.

The children were again amazed by how quickly the plant magic worked here in the Fairy Herb Garden. At home it might have taken a whole day for the plantain to pull the splinters up far enough that they could get at them with tweezers. Here it only took a few minutes before they were able to remove the poultices and carefully pluck each of the remaining devil's club thorns.

"Oh, ahhhhhhhh!" sighed the troll. "That feels so much better. Thank you, thank you!"

"Do you remember a part of the riddle?" Camie asked eagerly. She loved the riddles the trolls gave them to figure out their names. It was fun to try to guess what they meant.

"Hmmmmm," said the troll. "Well, yes. Yes. I am remembering something." He sounded surprised. "My name," he said tentatively. "My name begins with the opposite of out?" He said it like a question. "It does?" he wondered aloud. "Well, I guess it must." He was still amazed that he didn't know his own name, and was really hoping the children would help him remember it.

Camie laughed at this little dialogue the troll was having with himself. "Let's see," she said. "The opposite of out. That would be in, I bet. Your name must start with I...n..."

CHAPTER 4
Making Medicine

The new troll smiled at Camie. He felt excited that she had figured out the clue, and that he might find out his name again soon. "You are a clever child, aren't you?" he said.

Camie glowed with pride at the compliment.

"Well," said Trust, "Awareness and I will leave you to your healing work, children. I can see you've got things well in hand. We'll go back and see if we can help the fairies with the maypole."

"Thank you for your help," Sarah said. The children waved as the two trolls headed back to the Fairy Herb Garden.

"Now, how else can we help you?" Tago asked the troll eagerly.

"We'll only find out the rest of the riddle as you get better." Rowan yawned. It had been a big day and he was getting tired.

The troll collapsed in another fit of coughing before he could reply.

Their desire to help the troll gave the children energy. "I'm pretty sure plantain can help with coughs," said Hailey. "Isn't that right, Tago?"

Tago scratched his head. "You know," he said, "I can't seem to remember."

"Oh no!" said Rowan. "Viola and Stellaria both knew everything about their plants' healing qualities."

"Maybe this means the plant magic is fading more and more," said Sarah, sounding worried.

"Yikes!" wailed the troll. "I've got to go to the bathroom!" He jumped up and ran into the forest.

"Oh, I hope he comes back," said Hailey.

"Don't worry," soothed Rowan. "I think he will. Now, what do you girls think about using plantain to cure the cough?"

"My mom always gives me cough syrup when I have a cough," said Sarah. "The red stuff in the bottles from the store. It tastes good," she said, remembering the berry flavoring.

"Well," reasoned Rowan, "a syrup might be a good idea. What do you think, Hailey?"

"I think it's a good idea," Hailey replied. "I'm pretty sure I've heard of plantain being used for coughs even though it's not what we usually use at home, and syrups are great for healing coughs and sore throats."

"Oh," said Tago, "I do know how to make a syrup from plantain."

"Let's try it!" said Camie, clapping her hands.

The children followed Tago into his plantain house, but Hailey kept looking anxiously into the darkness of the forest. "What if he can't find his way back?" she asked, pulling on her brother's sleeve to get his attention.

Rowan looked down at his little sister. "Don't worry," he said.

"That troll is not being careful at all about where he walks. I'll be able to track him, no problem, if he doesn't come back."

Hailey smiled. She knew Rowan would be able to find that troll. She'd seen him track a deer through the woods with what he'd learned at wilderness school. "It sounds like Tago can help make the syrup, so I'll just keep watch at the window," she said. "So he doesn't think we've all gone away if he does come back." Hailey rested her head on the windowsill. She was sleepy and her eyes kept closing, but she was determined to keep watching for the troll.

"Good idea," said Camie, turning to look around Tago's home. It was very different from Viola's colorful place. Tago's home was simple, but comfortable. She saw his fairy bed made from twigs and stuffed with plantain leaves to form a mattress. He had a chair similarly made, and a simple kitchen set up. All around them were the oval leaves of plantain plants. Their green color and white parallel veins made nice walls and arched over their heads to form a sort of roof.

Tago walked to the kitchen area to get his mortar and pestle. "Here," he said. "Let's fill this with plantain leaves. We'll need the juice to make a syrup."

All the children began gathering leaves

from the plantain plants. It was easy to pick leaves that were not part of Tago's walls or roof. They simply picked the leaves at their base further back, and pulled them through the leaves in front and into the house. Rowan showed Sarah and Camie how when you picked a plantain leaf you could see little stretchy strands inside the leaf. "That's one way you can tell it's really plantain," he said.

Both girls were interested in this type of information. Their families didn't use plants for medicine like Rowan and Hailey's did, but after seeing all the healing that was possible with the chickweed and violets on their last adventures to the Fairy Herb Garden, they were both excited to learn more. Sarah had already begun introducing plant medicine to her family.

Once they'd gathered enough leaves, Rowan began mashing them in the mortar and pestle. Since it was fairy sized he knew they would have to make several batches in order to get enough juice to make a syrup for the troll.

Camie and Rowan took turns mashing up the leaves while Sarah pulled out her sketch pad. She began drawing the plantain plant. She'd decided to keep a journal of all the plants she learned about on these trips into the herb garden. That way she would remember what she was learning and could teach her family about it.

Sarah loved to draw, and she was careful to include all the things she'd learned about how to identify plantain. She drew the oval leaves tapering down at the base of the plant. She drew the parallel veins on the leaves that started right down where the leaves met the soil and spread out further up as the leaves got wider. She even drew a leaf separated from the plant so that she could include those stretchy strands that Rowan had told her about.

"He's back!" Hailey shouted, startling everyone. "The troll is back!"

"Why don't you run out and greet him, so he doesn't wonder where we are," Rowan encouraged.

"By myself?" Hailey looked frightened.

"I'll come with you, Hailey," Sarah said, smiling and taking her hand. The two girls hurried outside to greet the troll.

"Feeling better?" Sarah asked so the troll would hear her. She knew it would be hard for the troll to see them since they were so small and it was dark outside.

"Oh, there you are," he said, relieved. "I thought maybe I hadn't remembered my way back after all."

"The others are in the house making a syrup for your cough," Sarah explained.

"Thank you," said the troll. "It is hard to concentrate when I keep coughing so much, and now I've got to go to the bathroom all the time. My stomach hurts so much." The troll began coughing again and holding his belly.

"Here," said Sarah, "why don't you sit down." She showed him a soft, mossy place next to a nearby tree.

The troll lowered himself gratefully onto the moss, smiling sheepishly at the girls.

Sarah looked him over as he leaned back against the tree trunk. "You look awfully thin," she said. "How long have you been sick like this?"

The troll furrowed his brow, trying to remember. "Hmmmm," he said. "Seems like forever."

"Once we get rid of his cough," Sarah said, "I think we better see if plantain can help with diarrhea."

"Ewww," said Hailey, wrinkling up her nose. "I hate when I get that!" she added quickly, seeing the troll's look of worry at having disgusted her.

Just then Rowan, Camie, and Tago came out, carrying fairy bowls filled with plantain syrup.

The troll began coughing again when he saw them.

Rowan held the bowl up to the troll with both hands. The troll reached down and carefully grasped the tiny bowl between two of his fingers. He lifted it to his mouth and poured it in.

"Ah," he said. "That feels good on my throat. It's so sweet. It tastes good!"

Sarah smiled again, remembering the sweet taste of her own cough syrup.

"We added honey!" Camie said, holding up a second bowl of the precious liquid.

The troll swallowed the second bowlful and then jumped up and ran again into the forest.

"Where'd he go?" asked Camie. "He didn't tell us the next part of the riddle."

"He has diarrhea," Hailey explained.

"Ewwww," said Camie.

"Hailey, do you know if plantain helps with diarrhea?" Sarah asked.

CHAPTER 5
The Final Clues

By the time the troll returned a second time, Tago and the children already had a plantain infusion steeping in Tago's house. They were feeling more awake now, and kind of excited to be up so late in the night. It was fun working by moonlight. Hailey had recommended an infusion as the best way to use plantain to help with the diarrhea.

As the troll emerged from the woods he called excitedly to the children. "I've remembered something else," he said.

"Another part of the riddle?" Camie asked eagerly.

"Yes, yes!" he said. "I'm always at the beginning of things." He said it quickly as if he was afraid that he would forget it again before he was able to tell the children.

"Hmmmm. Always at the beginning of things and starts with In...." Camie trailed off, thinking hard. "In...side," she muttered. "In...jury? Indian? None of the words I can think of make any sense," she complained.

"Nope, me either," said Sarah.

The troll looked disappointed. Maybe the children wouldn't be able to figure out his name after all.

"Don't worry," said Rowan. "There's still one more clue. I'm sure of it. Once we cure your diarrhea you'll remember!"

At the mention of diarrhea the troll ran again into the forest.

"Gosh, I hope that infusion works," said Hailey. "He seems really miserable, and did you notice how thin he is?"

When the troll returned the next time, the children brought out the plantain infusion. "At home we would have had to let this steep for at least four hours for it to be at full strength," said Hailey. "But Tago says that it doesn't take that long in the fairy garden." She and the other children held out the tiny fairy cups to the troll.

"What's this?" he asked.

"It's a plantain infusion," explained Sarah. "We think it will help cure your diarrhea."

The troll took the cups they offered and eagerly swallowed the tea inside. When he'd finished, he leaned back against the tree and closed his eyes.

"Did it work? Did it?" Tago asked.

"Ahhhh, yes," he said after a few minutes. "I think it's going to do the trick. I'm feeling much better already."

"Can you remember the last part of the riddle?" Camie asked.

"Let me think," said the troll, closing his eyes once more. The children waited silently, tense with anticipation of their final clue.

The troll didn't open his eyes but he began to speak. "Let's see... Ah, yes, that's it... Some see how spirit is almost part of my name and claim I come from spirit, but many say a muse will bring my name to you."

"What's a muse?" Hailey asked, as the children circled up to try to figure out the riddle.

"Oh," said Sarah, "a muse gives writers and artists their ideas.

One of my teachers was telling me about Salvador Dali, he's a famous artist, and how he believed all his ideas for his paintings came from a muse."

"Hmmmm," said Rowan. "Idea starts with "i," ideas are at the beginning of things, and a muse gives artists their ideas. Maybe his name is Idea."

"Wasn't his name supposed to start with 'In'?" asked Hailey.

"Yes, and what did he mean when he said some see how spirit is almost part of his name?" asked Sarah.

"Oh," said Camie, "I think I know. My mom and I were just talking about this the other day when my sister and I were putting on a play for my parents. We couldn't think of what to make the play about, and she said we needed to look for some inspiration. She said to look around the house for something that made us think of a story we could act out... Inspiration! Don't you see? It starts with 'In,' the middle part sounds kinda like spirit, we needed it at the beginning of making our play, and I bet that's what muses bring to artists."

"Wow, Camie! Good job," said Rowan. "I bet you're right. Why don't you ask the troll if that's his name?"

Camie hurried over to the troll. "Is your name Inspiration?" she asked.

The troll smiled, and he said the word again out loud. "Inspiration... Yes! That is my name. How clever of you. You've figured it out!" The troll was very happy to have his name back. He sat for a moment repeating it quietly to himself. "Inspiration...Inspiration." As he did, his eyes came to rest on a patch of pansies not far away. The flowers stirred something inside of him. "My garden!" he exclaimed. "You must come with me to my garden."

The troll led them into the forest. The children and Tago followed eagerly, hopeful that Inspiration was leading them to the locked-up plantain magic. Even at fairy size the children found they could keep up with him easily. He was walking very slowly even though he seemed anxious to get back to his garden.

"Yikes," he gasped. "I'm so weak."

"I think you need to eat something," said Sarah. "You've been sick for a long time."

Hailey spotted some chickweed along the path and offered a handful of it to the troll. "Chickweed is really good to eat first thing after being sick," she said, "and it's my favorite green." She smiled and popped a bit into her mouth.

Tago flew forward with some plantain leaves. "These have a lot of vitamins and minerals in them," he said. "We always put them in our spring fairy salads."

Inspiration took the food gratefully. "I do feel better," he said. "It's amazing to eat and have it stay in my belly, but I'm awfully tired."

"Me too," yawned Hailey. That yawn set all the children to yawning, and suddenly they realized how very sleepy they were.

"I think we all better rest a while," said Inspiration. "We'll have to get back to my garden in the morning."

They found a nice, soft mossy area among the roots of a tree and cuddled up next to each other and slept.

As the sun rose, bringing a rosy dawn light to the forest, they woke up and rubbed their eyes. Tago had hardly slept he was so excited about his magic being restored. The children found him talking with another fairy they hadn't met before. She had the dark skin of an American Indian and wore a dress of deep green with serrated edges. The dress looked prickly and sparkled in a way that made the children wary of getting near her. Tago introduced her as Urtica, the nettle fairy.

Urtica smiled at the children and offered them each a small bowl filled with steamed nettles. She had one for Inspiration as well. "Tago was telling me that you would probably be hungry this morning," she explained.

The children took the food gratefully. They were hungry.

"I don't usually like steamed nettle very much," Hailey admitted, picking up the leaves in her fingers and dropping them back into the little bowl.

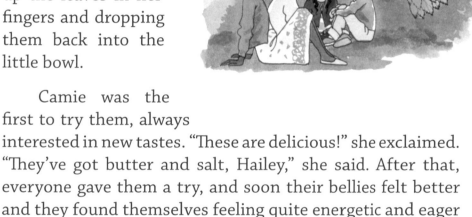

Camie was the first to try them, always interested in new tastes. "These are delicious!" she exclaimed. "They've got butter and salt, Hailey," she said. After that, everyone gave them a try, and soon their bellies felt better and they found themselves feeling quite energetic and eager to get moving.

They thanked Urtica for the breakfast and started down the path. They all moved faster in the morning light, though they stopped occasionally to pick some ripe salmonberries they found along the way. As they got further from the Fairy Herb Garden and the magic there, the children began to grow, and they could more easily reach the berries when they reached troll size.

Before long, they came to a little, arched wooden bridge that spanned a trickling creek. The bridge was a bit worn down, with some of the railing dangling from one side. The children moved across it carefully, testing the boards to be sure they would support their weight.

When they'd crossed the bridge, they found themselves on a little path leading to a simple wooden cottage tucked in a grove of cedar trees. Hailey noticed that there had once been a garden on either side of the path. There were still some pretty flowers blooming, but the plants were overrun with weeds and many of them looked droopy and unhealthy.

Inspiration dropped to his knees and began to run his hands up the stems of some of the healthier-looking plants, cradling the flowers that bloomed there. A tear ran down his cheek.

CHAPTER 6
A Magic Surprise

Inspiration wiped away the tear and moved to one corner of the garden, where he began to dig with his hands. Rowan saw a shovel standing next to the little cottage and ran to get it for the troll. He had a feeling he was digging for a very important treasure chest. With the help of the shovel, it wasn't long before Inspiration was lifting the little chest out of the earth. He cradled it in his arms and sat down at the garden's edge.

"Do you know how to open it?" Tago asked, unable to stay still. He could feel his plant's magic through the wood of the chest and was eager to release it.

"I bet we need to tend your garden," said Sarah quietly. "For Trust we wove, and for Awareness we told a story. Your passion is gardening, though, right?"

Inspiration nodded his head. "Yes," he said. "Yes, I think you're right. As we work together to bring life back to this place, the magic will be released."

All the children had helped their parents in the gardens at their houses before, so they knew what to do. They began pulling out weeds and clearing the area around the garden plants. Hailey, not liking to get her dress dirty, found a watering can and began giving each of the plants a drink. Rowan cleared around the peas. They were his favorite vegetable, and it was fun to find some healthy green pods that he could snack on while he worked. Sarah cleared around a patch of summer squash. They weren't ready to harvest yet, but she looked forward to them every year. Camie cleared around the kale, and Tago made sure one little patch of plantain had room to spread.

Inspiration smiled when he saw what Tago was doing. Always before he would have weeded the plantain out of his garden, but he knew he'd never be able to do that again after all the help that plant had offered him.

As each area of the garden was restored, the little chest began to shake and rattle, and finally the lid flew back. A swirl of green sparkles poured from the chest, filling the air with the gentle, green smell of plantain. Tago began to glow and sparkle as his magic returned to him. As the magic swirled out of the garden it attracted the other fairies and trolls.

Trust and Awareness came and joined hands with Inspiration. The three trolls stood together in Inspiration's garden and the most amazing thing happened. The garden was suddenly restored to its full beauty. The plants and flowers perked up, and blossoms opened and began dancing in the gentle spring breeze. The smell of all the blooms intertwined and wrapped the crowd in the sweet aroma of spring beauty.

All of the forest seemed to be waking up and celebrating the new breath of life that swept through the trees. The birds began to sing and even the creek seemed to trickle more happily over the rocks, adding its music to the bird chorus. The children each took a deep breath, smiling at the beautiful scents that filled their noses. And the fairies? Well, they looked around in wonder, eyes wide with delight. They began hugging one another and flying from plant to plant, touching the vibrant green leaves, sniffing the blossoms, caressing the flower petals.

With the healing of these three troll magic keepers, the spring magic had returned to the world, and everything felt new and fresh once more.

Somewhere, deep in the forest, in a tiny cottage, the May Queen opened her eyes. She smiled her beautiful smile at the Old Man of the Forest before settling back into her deep, deep slumber. The old man wept when she fell back into her sleep, but there were tears of happiness mixed in with his sorrow. He could feel the magic moving through his beloved trees, and for the first time in ever so long, he felt hope well up inside him, and it brought a smile to his weathered, wrinkled face.

At this moment, each of the fairies had a flash of the May Queen in their mind's eye. They saw her crowned in flowers and wearing her glittering, glowing rainbow cloak. The vision inspired laughter, acrobatics, and dancing. The three trolls stood together, delighted, as the fairies' spring festival impromptu grande finale performance took shape right there in Inspiration's beautiful garden.

The children stood, mesmerized by the beauty of the grand fairy dance, and happy inside that they had helped to make this moment possible. How very exciting it was to be part of these Fairy Garden adventures. They were glad that even when they returned home they were surrounded by the same plants they found here, and that they could call on the plant magic whenever they needed it.

Before long, the fairies began to drift happily and sleepily back to the fairy garden. Many of them had been up all night talking, dancing, and cleaning up from the festival. Tago, Viola, and Stellaria stayed to give a special thank-you to the children for their help in restoring the spring magic, and each of the trolls gave the children a grateful hug.

Then Inspiration reached into the treasure chest and pulled out a packet of seeds for each of the children and a special flower crown for Hailey. The trolls gathered around her as Inspiration placed it on her head. "Hailey," he said, "please accept this gift from us. Will you be our magic keeper among the humans?" he asked.

Hailey felt that beautiful crown on her head and nodded happily. She'd noticed that the flowers were from some of her favorite healing plants, calendula, monarda, chamomile, rose... She felt like she was wearing a crown of her best friends. "Rowan, I get to be a magic keeper!" she said happily.

"What does that mean?" Rowan asked Awareness. He was wondering just what his little sister was agreeing to.

"To be a magic keeper, Hailey, you will tell the stories of the trolls to your friends. This will help restore our magic in your world. I'm afraid trolls have gotten a rather bad rap among your kind since we've been sick."

Hailey laughed when she thought of all the troll stories she'd heard. Trolls were always ugly and mean, often hiding under bridges and keeping people from crossing. She liked the idea of telling stories about how trolls really were beautiful and clever and funny, though she wasn't sure anyone would believe her.

"The flowers on your crown will stay healthy and vibrant as long as you are telling our story," said Inspiration. "They'll also make your healing abilities stronger. If they start to wilt, they'll remind you."

"Why does Hailey get to be the magic keeper?" asked Camie. "I want to tell troll stories too."

"You can certainly tell troll stories, Camie. Every story will help. And you will get to be a magic keeper too, for one of the other magical races," Awareness explained. "Right now, though, it's Hailey's turn."

Hailey looked at each of the trolls. She loved them. She loved their cozy cottages, their weaving and story sticks and gardens. She would love to tell their stories. She touched the crown on her head again, smiled, and twirled happily on her ballerina tiptoes. Then she yawned and rubbed her eyes.

Her yawn was contagious and all the other children followed her example. After all, it had been a busy adventure and they'd only had a few hours of sleep.

"Tago, you better get these kids home. They look exhausted," said Stellaria.

Tago sprinkled the children with fairy dust and they found themselves sliding out from the tunnel slide at the yellow playground, the busyness of the Farmers' Market surrounding them. The four friends hugged each other tight before running off to find their parents to ask if they could go on home.

All of their parents were surprised when their children asked to go to bed early that night, and by how well they slept, so late into the following morning. Not one of them could ever guess the real reason their children were so tired or why they were so happy the following day, playing out among the blooming flowers.

Glossary

Tago (ta-go) Name of the plantain fairy, based on the scientific genus name of the plantain plant which is Plantago.

Urtica (ur-ti-kă): Name of the nettle fairy and also the scientific genus name of the nettle plant.

What's Next?

Learn more about plantain in the Herb Fairies member area!

After you complete the Magic Keeper's Journal, color Tago, make some recipes, and print out a picture of him for your wall. Learn lots more about plantain in Herbal Roots Zine, which has recipes, puzzles, activities, stories, songs and more!

Who's next?

Meet... ⟶

Herb Fairies

Melissa is the Lemon Balm Fairy. Join her in

Book Four: Treasure by Hopping Frog Pond.

Author Kimberly Gallagher, M.Ed. is also creator of *Wildcraft!, An Herbal Adventure Game*, by LearningHerbs.com. Her Masters in Education is from Antioch University in Seattle, and she taught at alternative schools in the Puget Sound region. Kimberly has extensive training in non-violent communication and conflict resolution. Her love of nature, writing, teaching, gardening, herbs, fantasy books and storytelling led her to create Herb Fairies.

Download Herb Fairies coloring pages in the member area.

Not a member? Visit HerbFairies.com.